Little Gil

zzz zzz zzz

Canadian Cataloguing in Publication Data
Papineau, Lucie
[Petit Gilles. English]
Little Gil

Translation of: Petit Gilles
ISBN 1-894363-77-9

I. Homel, David II. Beshwaty, Steve III. Title.

PS8581.A6658P4713 2001   jC843'.54
C2001-900298-X
PZ7.P2114Li2001

The use of any part of this publication, reproduced, transmitted in any form or by any means, electronic, mechanical, photocopying, recording or otherwise, or stored in a retrieval system, without the prior consent of the publisher is an infringement of the copyright law.

© Les éditions Héritage inc. 2001
All rights reserved.

Publisher: Dominique Payette
Series Editor: Lucie Papineau
Art direction and design: Primeau & Barey

Legal Deposit: 3rd Quarter 2001
Bibliothèque nationale du Québec
National Library of Canada

Dominique & Friends
Canada:
300 Arran Street, Saint-Lambert, Quebec,
Canada J4R 1K5

USA:
P.O. Box 800
Champlain, New York
12919

Tel: 1 888 228-1498
Fax: 1 888 782-1481
E-mail:
dominique.friends@editionsheritage.com

Printed in Canada
10 9 8 7 6 5 4 3 2

The publisher wishes to thank the Canada Council for its support, as well as SODEC and Canadian Heritage.

Government of Quebec – Book Publication
Tax Credit Program – SODEC

To Florence, who loves the color of words...
L.P.

For Tintin-Justin!
S.B.

Little Gil

Story: Lucie Papineau
Illustrations: Steve Beshwaty

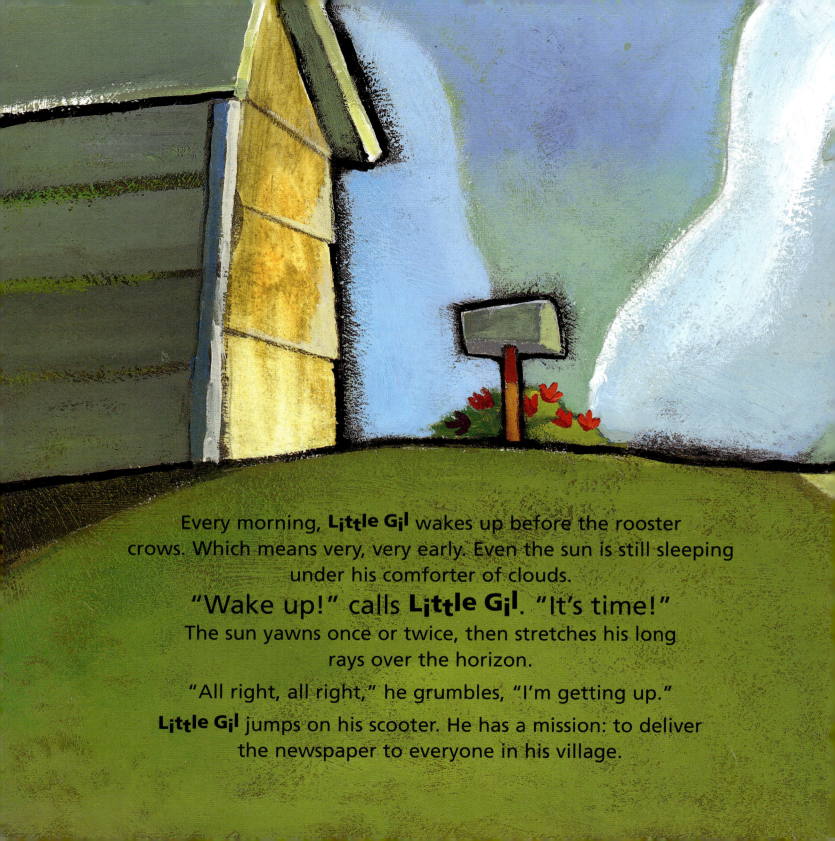

Every morning, **Little Gil** wakes up before the rooster crows. Which means very, very early. Even the sun is still sleeping under his comforter of clouds.

"Wake up!" calls **Little Gil**. "It's time!"

The sun yawns once or twice, then stretches his long rays over the horizon.

"All right, all right," he grumbles, "I'm getting up."

Little Gil jumps on his scooter. He has a mission: to deliver the newspaper to everyone in his village.

Little Gil goes speeding off. At the first bend, he comes to Mr. Gerrard's house with its shutters painted all the colors of the rainbow. Suddenly **Little Gil** hears someone calling. "Help! Munchka climbed up the tree and she can't get down!"

Poor Mr. Gerrard! And poor Munchka!
She's trembling like a leaf among the apples.
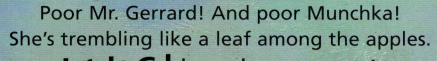 has the answer!

He scoots back to his house and returns, carrying a heavy book with a bright blue cover.

"Jump, Munchka, you can do it! If you jump, you can have this book. It's a love story, and it's 800 pages long!"

Those are the magic words! Munchka grabs a branch, dangles her feet in thin air and drops onto the grass. Then she rushes right for the book.

Mr. Gerrard is delighted. To thank Little Gil, he invites him to have a cup of tea, and as many marshmallow cookies as he can eat. Meanwhile, Munchka is lost in her book.
"I'd better get going," Little Gil says, jumping on his scooter.
"I have a mission."

At the top of the hill, he comes to his second house, the one with the pointed roof and the round windows.

"Help!" someone calls, "bullfrogs have taken over my living room."

Little Gil scoots into the room.

Miss Pimms, looking as green as frog skin, is hanging from the chandelier. Good thing **Little Gil** has an idea.

On wings of courage, he catches the world's biggest housefly. Then he ties it to the end of a stick. Now he's ready to go bullfrog fishing. At the end of its string, the fly soars over the battalion of frogs.

"Hey, boys," says their chief, "did you see that enormous, juicy, scrumptious fly?"

Once he has their attention, **Little Gil** backs out the door and into the yard, leading every single frog out of the house. Bang! Miss Pimms slams her door shut.

To thank **Little Gil**, she gives him a yoga class in her suddenly serene living room. Meanwhile, the bullfrogs croak at the door, but no one will let them in. "I've got to be going," **Little Gil** says, jumping back on his scooter. "I have a mission."

By the riverbank, Little Gil comes to a house that looks as though it's growing in a tree. That's where Lulee lives. She's his next stop.
"Help!" calls Lulee,
"I've been kidnapped by the Kruktuks!"
Little Gil climbs up towards his friend's voice. And there on the roof, among the branches, what does he see?
The Kruktuks, dancing their dance, and singing out their name.

"It must be a trap,"

Little Gil decides. "If I go into their tent, the Kruktuks will capture me and I'll never get out."

But Lulee is already a prisoner. And to be a prisoner with Lulee is certainly better than anything else he can think of.

Good thing **Little Gil** comes to his senses. On wings of courage, he runs to the riverbank. He kneels down in the wet grass and starts searching as hard as he can.

The sun is starting to wonder what's going on when **Little Gil** finally finds the needle in the haystack: a real, live five-leaf clover.

He climbs back up to see the Kruktuks.

"I'll give you this five-leaf clover if you set Lulee free!" he says bravely.

The Kruktuks stop singing their terrible song. Their eyes grow as wide as the full moon. For them, the five-leaf clover is a magical charm!

With their eyes on the five-leaf clover, the Kruktuks forget all about their prisoner. **Little Gil** opens the door to the tent and Lulee leaps into his arms. "You're not a moment too soon," she says.

All afternoon, they play games together. And that's better than anything else he can think of.

By the time **Little Gil** goes home,
the sun is almost at the end of his day's work.
"Mission accomplished,"
Little Gil says proudly. "Everyone in the
village got their... Darn it, the newspapers!
I forgot to deliver them!"

Little Gil jumps back
on his scooter with his papers
for everyone in the village.
"Be quick,"
says the sun, yawning,
"I've got other places to go."

But what does **Little Gil** hear at the first bend?
"Help! Munchka climbed up on the roof and she can't get down!"

Today, the sun will just have to work overtime…